TWO BEARS

and *Joe*

To my grandson Jacob
P.L.

To Laura Cecil
J.O.

VIKING/PUFFIN
Published by the Penguin Group
Penguin Books Ltd, 27 Wrights Lane, London W8 5TZ, England
Penguin Books USA Inc., 375 Hudson Street, New York, New York 10014, USA
Penguin Books Australia Ltd, Ringwood, Victoria, Australia
Penguin Books Canada Ltd, 10 Alcorn Avenue, Toronto, Ontario, Canada M4V 3B2
Penguin Books (NZ) Ltd, 182–190 Wairau Road, Auckland 10, New Zealand

Penguin Books Ltd, Registered Offices: Harmondsworth, Middlesex, England

First published by Viking 1995
1 3 5 7 9 10 8 6 4 2

Published in Puffin Books 1997
1 3 5 7 10 8 6 4 2

Text copyright © Penelope Lively, 1995
Illustrations copyright © Jan Ormerod, 1995

Made and printed in Italy by printers srl – Trento

British Library Cataloguing in Publication Data

A CIP catalogue record for this book is available from the British Library

ISBN 0–670–86060–3 Hardback
ISBN 0–140–55551–X Paperback

TWO BEARS
and *Joe*

Penelope Lively

Illustrated by Jan Ormerod

Puffin
Viking

One morning when Joe woke up,
there were two bears in his room.
His mother couldn't see the bears
and his father couldn't see the bears.
Joe and the bears played bear games
with the bedclothes and then his
mother said, "That's enough messing
about, Joe. It's time for breakfast."

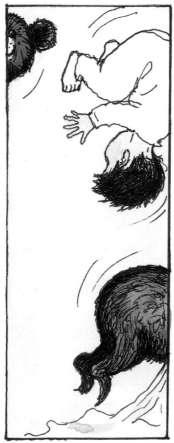
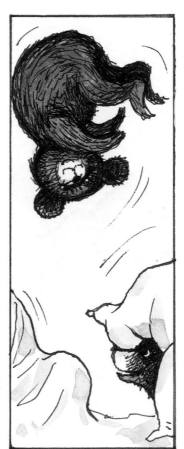

Joe shared his breakfast with the bears.
There was a black bear and there was a
brown bear. The bears sat under the table
and made growly noises. Joe's mother still
couldn't see the bears but she could hear
them.

"Not so much noise, Joe, please. And don't
keep dropping your toast on the floor," she
said.

"Now what?" said the brown bear.

"Now whatever you like," said Joe.

"We like climbing trees," said the black bear.

"There isn't a tree in my house," said Joe.

"Oh, yes there is," said the bears. "Look!
Race you to the top!"

They climbed and they jumped and they slid
and they swung. Sometimes Joe caught the bears
and sometimes the bears caught Joe. And then from
far away and down below they heard someone calling.

"What are you doing, Joe?"
said Joe's father.

"Uh-oh . . ." said the bears. "Trouble.
Put away the tree, quick!"

"And where on earth have all those
leaves come from, I'd like to know?"
said Joe's father.

"Oops!" said the brown bear. "He nearly saw us then! Tell you what – we need some snow now."

"No snow in this house," said Joe.

"Oh, yes there is," said the black bear. "Feel!"

They whooshed and they whumped in the snow, and they slithered and they slipped. Joe pushed the bears over and the bears pushed Joe over. And then from miles and miles away they heard someone calling.

"What are you doing, Joe?" said his mother.

"Uh-oh . . ." said the bears.
"Better roll up the snow. Quick!"

Joe's mother said, "It's time for lunch, Joe. I wonder why it feels so cold in here?"

At lunch-time the bears hid under the table again.

"Has she seen us?" said the brown bear.

"Not yet," said Joe. And he gave the bears
 some of his lunch.

"We like you," said the bears.

"I like you back," said Joe.
"What shall we do this afternoon?"

"This afternoon we'll go fishing in the river,"
said the black bear.

"No fishing here," said Joe. "No river."

"Oh, yes there is," said the brown bear. "Jump in!"

They sploshed and they splashed and they dipped
and they dived. They didn't catch any fish
but they had a good time. And then from over the hills
and beyond the trees they heard someone calling.

"What are you doing, Joe?" said his father.

"Quick – pour away the river!"said the black bear.

"And why are there wet footmarks all over the floor?"
said Joe's father.

"Uh-oh . . ." said the brown bear. "He's going
to see us. Quick – hide in the cave!"

"Just where are you off to, Joe?" said his
father.

But Joe was deep down in the bears' cave
with the black bear and the brown bear.
It was snug and dark and earthy in the cave.
They hid and they pounced and they booed
and they bounced. And then from far away
and up above in the world, they heard
someone calling.

"Where are you, Joe?" said his mother. "It's time for bed."

"Got to go now," said Joe. "See you another day."

"See you another day," said the bears.

So Joe came up from the cave and his mother said,
"There you are! Wherever have you been,
and who were you talking to?"

"Nowhere, really," said Joe. "Nobody, really."

"And how did you get so dirty?" said his mother.

"Can't remember," said Joe.

He had a specially long bath. He scrubbed his face
and his hands and his fur and his paws until he was
as clean as clean could be.

And then he went to bed and
slept as sound as a bear in a cave.

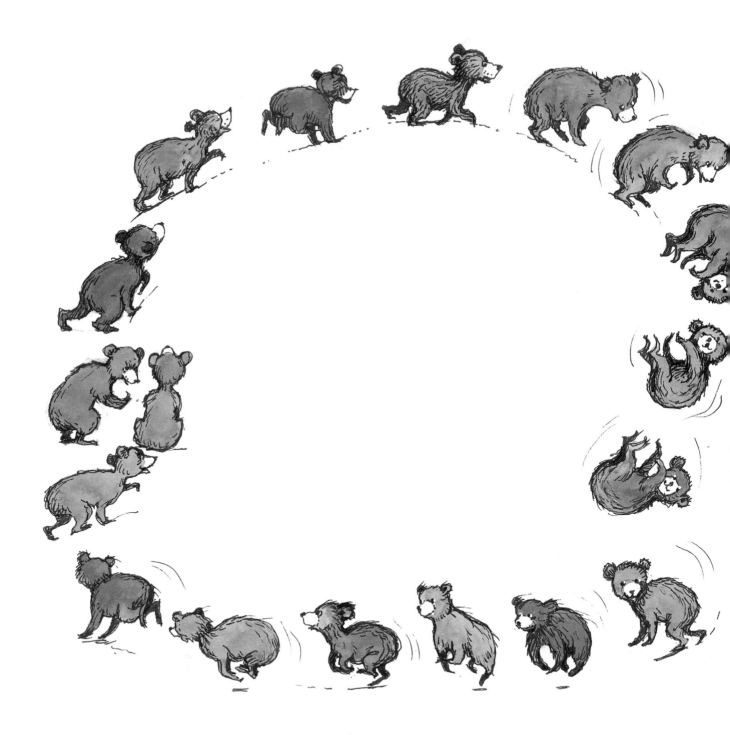